To Caz and Helen, Clare and Julia, Amelia, Liz, and Ben • with my love and thanks for all your help H.C. •

454 2102

First U.S. edition 1995

Library of Congress Cataloging-in-Publication Data

Craig, Helen.
Charlie and Tyler at the seashore / Helen Craig.—1st U.S. ed.
Summary: While spending the day at the seashore, two adventurous mice share
a wild ride in a boat, become lost in a toy theater, and escape from a seagull's nest.
ISBN 1-56402-573-X
[1. Mice—Fiction.  2. Adventure and adventurers—Fiction.
3. Seashore—Fiction.  4. Cousins—Fiction.]  I. Title.
PZ7.C84418Cf    1995
[E]—dc20        94-24620

2 4 6 8 10 9 7 5 3 1

Printed in Italy

The pictures in this book were done in pen and ink and watercolor.

Candlewick Press
2067 Massachusetts Avenue
Cambridge, Massachusetts 02140

# CHARLIE AND TYLER AT THE SEASHORE

## HELEN CRAIG

CANDLEWICK PRESS
CAMBRIDGE, MASSACHUSETTS

One warm sunny day,
Charlie the country mouse
was sitting on the porch of
his comfortable home in the
hedgerow. He was reading
a letter from his cousin Tyler
the town mouse.
This is what it said:

Dear Charlie,
How's life with you?
As dull as ever, I bet.
Well, now's your chance to
do something exciting. Meet
me tomorrow at the old oak
tree an hour before sunrise
for A DAY AT THE SEASHORE!
Love, Tyler

"Oh, dear!" said Charlie.
"I don't want to do
something exciting.
I'm very happy here."
But the next morning he
got up while it was still
dark, shouldered his
old satchel, and set off
all the same.

Tyler was waiting for him
by the oak tree, rigged out
in a sailor's jersey and a
sea captain's hat.
"Ahoy there!" he called.
"Here comes Mrs. Pigeon.
She's going to give us a lift."

The sun was just rising as Mrs.
Pigeon set Charlie and Tyler down
on the seashore.
"Have a lovely day," she said. "And
don't forget, meet me on the cliff top
at sunset and I'll take you home."

They looked around them. Out of the mist loomed a big shape.
"It's a motorboat!" said Tyler. "Let's go for a trip. I'll be the captain
because I know about boats. Welcome aboard, Able Seaman Charlie."

Tyler looked around for the
controls, but he couldn't find any.
"Ah!" he said. "Just a small setback.
Let's wait until the mist clears."
So the two little mice settled down
in the cabin for a snooze.

They were woken by a loud
whirring noise.
"What's happening?" squeaked Charlie.
Waves were flashing past the windows.

"We're at sea—I think,"
said Tyler as the boat
lurched one way and
then the other.

"Can't you stop it?" Charlie
wailed. "You're the captain."
But Captain Tyler had no
idea *what* to do.

The two mice scrambled on deck and hung on tight. The boat was

speeding madly all by itself, backward and forward across the water.

They were frightened for their lives.

At last the boat hurtled toward the shore and hit a rock. Charlie and Tyler were catapulted into the air and landed—*SPLASH!*—in a shallow pool.

"Oh dear, oh dear," said Charlie.

But Tyler picked himself up and looked around.

"Let's go beachcombing," he said.
"What's beachcombing?" asked Charlie.
"It's looking for treasure and useful
things in the sand," Tyler replied,
marching off.

He soon found a
little sword that
had once belonged
to a toy soldier,
and a metal button
that made a
perfect shield.

Charlie found a parasol
and a little bell on a chain.
"This will be just right for
my front door," he said.
He was beginning to
enjoy himself. They set
off again, their bags laden
with treasure.

At last they found themselves under the pier.

"Hey, we can have some fun up there!" said Tyler. "It's only a little climb."

Charlie looked up with a sinking heart. But a great big dog was lolloping toward them. He had no choice but to follow.

Way down below, the waves splashed and the dog barked. "This is scary," said Charlie. "Nonsense!" said Tyler.

Underneath the floorboards of the pier they found a hole and squeezed through into a very strange place.

"Oh, Tyler!" said Charlie. "What HAVE you gotten us into now?"

They climbed on and up into a dimly lit room full of shadowy figures. "Where can we be?" whispered Charlie. All of a sudden, lights came on, a curtain went up, and music began to play. They were in a toy theater!

With a whirring of the cogwheels below, the little figures began to move in time to the music. Tyler and

Charlie pretended they were part of
the show, but too late—they'd been
seen. It was time for a quick exit.

"Phew!" puffed Tyler. "I'm hungry after all that. Let's find some food."

They had sausages, chips, popcorn, and a nice piece of caramel apple . . .

And they did very well when it came to ice cream.

They visited the aquarium
and the hall of mirrors.
All too soon it was time
to go and meet Mrs. Pigeon.

Up on the cliff they sat
and watched the boats
out at sea. Charlie liked
it. It was almost as
peaceful as his home
in the hedgerow.

Then a terrible thing happened.
A huge seabird swooped down and grabbed Tyler in her claws.
"Help! Help!" he squeaked. Charlie watched in horror as the
great bird carried Tyler far away.

Charlie began to cry. His eyes were so full of tears that he didn't see the bird turn in a circle and head back to her home under the cliff.

The bird dropped Tyler into the nest next to her
waiting chick, and flew off again. The chick was
always hungry and Tyler was to be its next meal.

The chick
moved closer
to Tyler.

It gave him a peck.

Tyler was furious
and drew his sword.

"Take that!"
he shouted.
"Ow!" squawked
the chick.

The awful noise they
made floated up to Charlie,
alone and sad on the cliff top.
He crept to the edge and
peeked over. He couldn't
believe his eyes.

"Hang on, Tyler!" he shouted.
"I'm coming!" He started off down
the cliff without a thought for the
dangers below, tumbling, bouncing,
and sliding, until he landed in a
small bush just above the nest.

Quickly he pulled the little bell from his satchel
and lowered it down above Tyler's head.
"Grab hold and I'll pull you up," he shouted.

Tyler swung dangerously over the sea. Charlie pulled as hard as he could.

The chick squawked, but by the time the mother bird came back, Tyler was gone.

Charlie and Tyler scrambled
to the top of the cliff where
Mrs. Pigeon found them later,
lying exhausted under some
large leaves.
"You poor things!" she cooed.
"You do look tired. Climb in
the mailbag and I'll fly
you home."

The two mice took a last
look at the seashore. It all
seemed so peaceful from
the air.
"Charlie, you're a hero," said
Tyler. "You saved my life."

It was night when Mrs.
Pigeon put them down
by the hedgerow.
"Good-bye and thanks,"
they called.

Safe and sound at Charlie's home, they sat on the porch
and talked over all that had happened.
"What a fine adventure we had!" said Tyler. Charlie wasn't so
sure. However, on one thing they did agree—they had both
been terribly, terribly BRAVE!

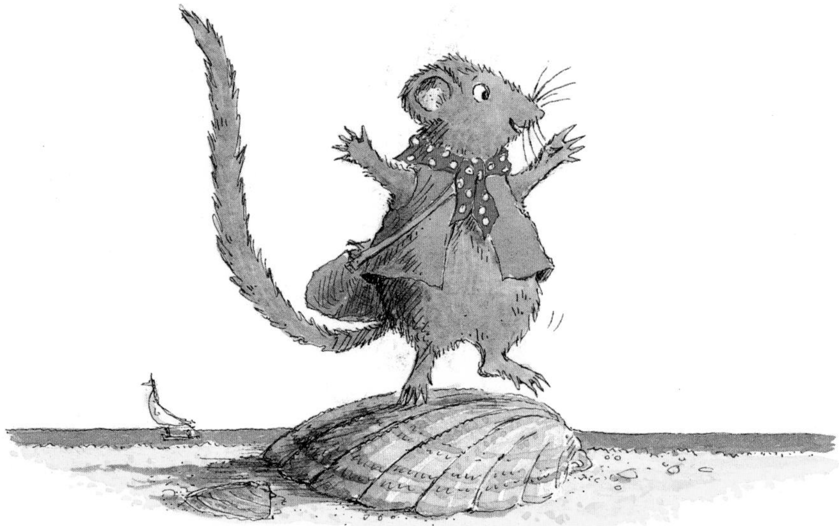